The Seal's Fate

First published in 2015 in Great Britain by
Barrington Stoke Ltd, 18 Walker Street, Edinburgh, EH3 7LP

www.barringtonstoke.co.uk

This story first appeared in a different form in *Thirteen*
(Orchard Books, 2005)

Text © 2005 Eoin Colfer
Illustrations © 2015 Victor Ambrus

A CIP catalogue record for this book is available from the British
Library upon request

ISBN: 978-1-78112-431-4

Printed in China by Leo

The Seal's Fate
EOIN COLFER

Illustrations by VICTOR AMBRUS

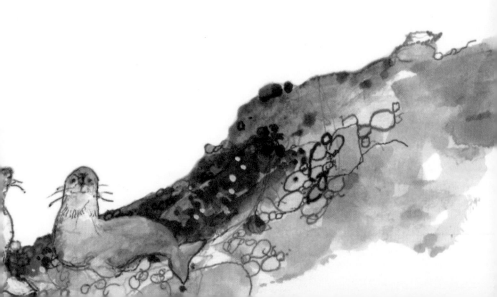

To all those who have jumped from the High Wall

CONTENTS

CHAPTER 1

Buddies

The baby seal looked at Bobby Parrish with round black eyes. Cute if you liked that sort of thing. If you were a girl maybe, with posters of Manga ponies on her walls. Boys didn't do cute. Boys caught fish and gutted them and fed their innards to the gulls. Boys killed things because that was how life was, and you'd better be ready for it when school was over. Bobby knew that when Saint Brendan's doors closed behind him for the last time he would strip off his uniform, put on some oilskins and take his berth on his dad's boat, *The Lady Irene*.

Still, the seal was cute. Bobby could admit that much to himself, as long as no one was around. He was careful not to think it too loud, in case one of his friends was telepathic. The animal's black nose quivered and white sunspots spread across its back like a mane. Cute. But, like Dad said, it was vermin.

Bobby crawled a couple of feet closer, careful not to startle the seal. Limestone crags pressed

into his stomach, and rock-pool slime destroyed his jeans. It didn't matter. A working man had to be able to ignore discomfort to get the job done.

The seal watched him. It was not afraid.

Quite the opposite – it seemed pleased at the prospect of company. It arched its back and slapped its flippers on the slick rock. Bobby slapped the rocks himself, to try to get a bit of rapport going with the seal. It seemed to do the trick. The seal stretched its tiny head forward, and coughed three short barks.

'We're friends now,' Bobby thought. 'Buddies. I bet this seal thinks we're going to spend the summer swimming around the bay, fighting crime.'

"Well, old buddy," Bobby told the seal, out loud. "Sorry to disappoint you, but your future is not going to be quite so rosy."

Bobby reached behind him and wrapped his fingers around the handle of the club.

CHAPTER 2

Rope Burns

Brian Parrish had spoken from the deck of *The Lady Irene*. The young people gathered around the quay walls above, hanging on his every word. The men never spoke to the boys down at the dock. This must be important.

Bobby thought his dad was like a different person when he was surrounded by sea and stone. He was

invincible, with wind lines burned into his face, and hands that could strangle a conger eel. Every step he took away from the sea seemed to make him smaller, until at home he would collapse into the armchair and have someone bring him his tea.

But here Bobby's dad was in his element, and everything about him was fierce.

"It's the seals, boys," he said. "They're a bloody plague."

He called them boys even though Babe Meara was in the group. Babe considered herself a boy, and anybody who suggested otherwise better have shin guards.

"I saw three today," Seanie Ahern cried. "Off the point."

"There were four!" Seán Ahern, his twin, corrected. "And they were in the bay!"

The Ahern twins would argue about the colour of mud. Their real names were Jesse and Randolph, but who would be mean enough to call them that. Only a parent who loved Western films.

Brian Parrish raised his hands for silence. The brown palms were criss-crossed with white rope burns and welts. Fishing was the most dangerous job in the world. Two of Brian's brothers hadn't been lucky enough to get off with just rope burns.

"The seals are everywhere," Brian said. "The

bay, the point, even poking their noses into the

dock, the cheeky buggers. They're infesting the

entire headland this year. A fellow I know from

Ross reckons they're thriving on all the effluent the

factories pump out."

The Ahern twins giggled and elbowed each other when they realised what effluent actually meant.

"I wouldn't mind that," Brian Parrish went on, "if they'd stick to eating waste, but those seals are eating our catch too, and they're ripping the nets apart."

Everybody knew what that meant. Holes in the nets led to long evenings weaving them back together, with sharp twine wearing grooves in your hands.

"Things are bad enough already this year, without having to put up with these vermin too," Brian said. "We haven't had a sniff of mackerel all summer and the crabs are either getting smart or scarce."

The other men nodded and muttered their agreement around roll-up cigarettes.

CHAPTER 3

Silver Seas

Everyone knew that hard times were upon them, no doubt about it.

Duncade was just about fished out, what with the factory trawlers and the Spanish boats that sneaked into Irish waters. Mackerel had always been the life's blood of the south-east. Now there were barely enough fish to bait the pots.

There hadn't been a silver sea in years. That
was a time when huge shoals of sprats – the
mackerel's meal of choice – swam along the coast
and often into the dock itself. When that happened

every man, woman and child was pressed into service, and every container from bucket to wash basket was lowered into the sea to trap the hungry silver-blue fish following the sprats.

"So, here's the way it's going to be," Brian Parrish said. "We're going to fight back. From this day on, there is a bounty on seals."

Bobby felt a jolt of electricity hop from kid to kid. A bounty meant money, and there is no better way to excite kids than with the promise of money.

"Anyone who brings in a seal's flipper gets a crisp pound note from me," Brian went on.

'A pound,' Bobby thought. 'That's an entire day's farm wages.' Then he thought of something else.

"A seal's flipper?" he said. "But that means you would have to ..."

"Kill it, son," his father said. His voice was flat. "Kill it dead, with rocks or clubs, I don't care. They are big rats and we will send them packing!"

The others were with Brian as the combination of bloodlust and riches sent their hearts racing. Seal bounty had been common 50 years ago. All their parents and grandparents had hunted the rocks for extra money. But there hadn't been a bounty in decades. It was most likely illegal now.

"I want you to find those big rats wherever they try to sun themselves," Brian Parrish said. "This summer you will be waiting whenever they poke their shiny heads above the waves. Waiting with something blunt to smite them. Do you hear me?"

The boys nodded, keen to appear casual before the fishermen. Real men of the sea did not get excited. A blue whale to rival Moby Dick could breach right off their bow, and a real fisherman would spit over the gunwales and pretend not to notice.

"We all know the spots where the seals go. Lure them in with a slab of cod, then let them have it with the club," Brian Parrish said. "Take care mind. A bull seal will take a chunk out of your leg with its teeth. Worse still, it will break your bones with a swipe of its tail."

Bobby felt his heart expand in his chest. He hoped its thumping would not shake his jacket. But he was not ready for all this talk of killing and breaking bones. It was too soon. He was just 13 years of age. Too young to smoke, but old enough to kill a seal. Bobby glanced around at his companions, Paudie, the twins and Babe Meara. Their eyes were alight. He tried to match their giddiness, for his father's sake.

His father stood there in command of the whole dock. Bobby realised that Brian Parrish was a leader to these men. They looked to him for example. It was a crippling year, and here hadn't Brian come up with a solution. His father felt the look and threw Bobby a wink.

"Be the first," that wink from his dad said. "Be the first to come to me with a seal's flipper."

Bobby winked back, and added in a grin, but it felt like a sticker, pasted over his real feelings.

He didn't want to kill a seal. He didn't know if he could.

CHAPTER 4

Toe in the Water

The seal's eyes were hypnotic, round, deep and black, as if they knew things that you never could.

'What have you seen?' Bobby wondered. 'Deep ocean reefs? Odd 8-legged creatures that could swallow a ship? Your family's blood spread across the flat rocks, washed away a little more with every lap of the tide?'

"Stop it," he hissed at the cub. "I know what you're doing. Trying to make yourself real to me. But it won't work. You're vermin. Nothing more. That's what Dad says, and who am I going to believe? You, a seal I never met before, or my own father?"

Bobby raised the club. It had been passed down his family to him. Bobby's grandfather had used it for general clubbing duties in the second half of the 1900s. Grandad had presented the grisly relic to Bobby when he heard about the seal bounty.

"I whittled this myself out of a lump of ebony that came off an African wreck," Grandad told him.

"It might be old but, by Jesus, you whack anything living with this and that's the end of the story. See this here ..."

Grandad pointed with a nicotine-brown finger to a splat patch on the club.

"That's from a shark that got caught up in the nets one time," he said. "I took one eye out of him and half his brain with a single whack. He survived, though."

Grandad had lost himself in the memory. He was gazing out to sea, looking at things only he could see.

"He's out there now," he said. "That shark. Half-blind and all mental. Waiting for me to put so much as a toe in the water." He handed Bobby the club. "It's all yours now, boy. Pull well back and follow through. Oh, and wear old clothes. When a seal's bowels go, they go everywhere."

CHAPTER 5

A Better Target

Bobby looked at the seal and ran his finger along the club's grip. A single strip of hide twisted six inches up the shaft. Grandad claimed to have stripped the hide from a rhino who ran into his Jeep when he was on safari. The rhino knocked itself clean out but it was alive in Africa still, just waiting

for Grandad to put so much as a toe inside Kenya ...
The strap felt more like lino than rhino to Bobby.

Bobby stood and took a step closer. Every step took him closer to the next part of his life.

Bobby's friends couldn't wait. They wanted to hop into adulthood, grins red with seal blood. Smoking would be next, then the boats, then weekends in the pub. Bobby wished there could be a part in-between. Maybe there had been once, but now the years were being worn away like soft rock. It was straight from childhood into adulthood now. No time for acne or moods.

Bobby held the club out in front of him. He spoke his grandad's words. "Pull well back and follow through." The seal followed the club with those big, wise eyes.

"It's not a fish," Bobby wanted to shout. "I'm going to kill you with this, so stop looking at it like it's your best friend." At that moment, Bobby hated the seal. He hated it for being so stupid and trusting – and for tearing nets.

Bobby took several breaths, steeling himself.

'It's an animal,' he told himself. 'Vermin. One blow and it's over. If you do it, you'll belong. Don't do it, and you'll be excluded for ever.'

The seal cub hoisted itself up on its front flippers, and bent its pointy head down. The perfect target. There would never be a better target. Bobby wrapped both hands around the club, and squeezed until the blood left his fingers. He lifted the club high over his head ...

CHAPTER 6

Skin Deep

Two Days Before

It had been Babe's idea to set up a practice area.
She was very bloodthirsty for a girl.

"Soldiers train for battle," Babe explained, as
she hung a melon in a home-made string harness

from a tree branch. "So we should get ready to hunt the enemy."

"Enemy?" Bobby said. He wasn't sure about this.

Babe turned on him. Her name didn't do her justice. Babe Meara was hard beyond her years, and aggressive beyond her size. Several local lads had misjudged Babe's nature and were now walking with limps.

"Yes, Parrish," she spat. "The enemy. Seals. You should know better than anyone. Your own dad's nets are taking the worst hammering. If I was you I'd be diving off the rocks with a knife, hunting those vermin down."

It could well be true. One time Babe had tracked down a dog who ate her cat. She got revenge for Mr Toodles with half a pound of steak stuffed with laxative pills.

Babe took a marker from her pocket and sketched a few marks on the melon. Round black eyes, a button nose and some whiskers.

Seán Ahern was a bit slow to catch on. "What is that? A cat?" he asked.

Babe threw the marker at him. "No, dimwit. It's obviously a seal. We're hunting seals, remember?"

Seán rubbed his head. "Oh yeah, seals. I see it now."

His brother Seanie chuckled. "A cat. Dimwit."

"Yeah, well," Seán said. "The nose threw me. It's kind of feline looking."

Babe set the melon swinging. Then she backed up a few steps and took a hurling stick from her belt. It was two feet long with wicked-looking metal bands criss-crossing the base.

This particular hurling stick was banned from every pitch in the south-east, but Babe kept it around because it was good and heavy and you never know when you might have to whack something.

She hefted the hurling stick like a mini ninja. "The way I see it," she said, "the little sod is lying on the flat rocks, tearing up a length of net."

Babe advanced step by step, walking sideways, with the hurling stick high behind her.

"So you come in slow," she said. "You never take your eyes off the ball ... melon ... I mean, head. The seal will be moving about a bit so you have to try and be ready."

Bobby tried to grin along with the rest of them, but he had always had a good imagination. He could see the seal. For him, the pale green melon had turned into a water-slick, deep brown head. The inked eyes sparkled and rolled. The ragged whiskers shivered in the breeze.

The smile on Bobby's face was only skin deep.

Babe froze two steps from the target. "This is the vital bit," she whispered. "This is when the seal could spot you. Then the bugger has two choices. One – he can run. Two – he can fight." She twirled her hurling stick in one hand. It cut the air with a gentle *whoosh*. "So you have to be ready for both."

With speed honed by years of standing up to taller people, Babe Meara took the final two steps. She brought her hurling stick down in a slice at the swinging fruit.

The first blow battered the melon from its harness of string.

The second shattered it into a million soggy pieces before it hit the ground.

"Jesus," Bobby blurted.

Babe grinned, as green melon juice spattered across her forehead.

"Will you look at him," she said. "He can't even stomach someone killing a piece of fruit. You'll never be able to handle an actual seal, Bobby."

The others laughed, and gave Bobby farmer slaps on the back.

"Go on, Bobby, you eejit," Seán said.

"Get a grip, Parrish," Seanie added. "It's a melon. You, on the other hand, are a lemon."

But Paudie, Bobby's closest friend in the group, went deeper. "Don't worry, pal. When the time comes Bobby Parrish will show us all. Isn't that right, Bobby. You'll show us."

Bobby looked Babe in the eye and tried to turn the situation round. "That's right," he said. "I'll show you."

Babe held out her hurling stick. "Why don't you start with a melon?"

CHAPTER 7

Don't Make Waves

As it happened, Bobby hadn't had to go next.

Paudie had grabbed the hurling stick and made a joke of the whole thing as he pranced around and put on a funny voice. In the end he struck his melon and stamped on the pieces.

It was funny enough to make Bobby see that the melon was only a melon, no matter the eyes, nose and whiskers that Babe had scrawled upon it. When his turn came, Bobby had driven the melon right out of its string harness. But it was only a melon, and it proved nothing.

Now things were different.

This was a real seal in front of Bobby, not a piece of fruit with a shell the same size as a seal's skull. And the real seal's head was not swaying to and fro in a gentle arc. It was cocked to one side, as the seal stared at the club raised over Bobby's head.

Bobby was sure his father had been disappointed in him, even though Brian Parrish hadn't said as much. Bobby had not been the first to bring in a seal's flipper. The smart money had been on Paudie, but Babe Meara had surprised them when she'd backed up her big mouth with action. She'd arrived at the dock two days after the melon practice run with a stroke of red on her shirt and a flipper in her hand. She'd tossed the flipper onto the flagstones where Brian Parrish was gutting pollock.

"Pound please," she'd said, in a low voice.

Brian had handed the pound over. Babe had taken it and shoved it deep in her jeans pocket. No gloating. Not a word. Then Babe had gone home,

and no one saw her for a couple of days. "She's got a bit of a chill," her mother said.

So now it was Bobby's turn. He had been doing his best to avoid seals, but this little fella had more or less jumped out of the sea into his lap. Grandad's club was raised over his head and there was only one way for it to go. Down.

Bobby could feel the strain in his arms. It was soon or never. He could see the dock's high wall beyond the arch of his body. There were a couple of lads walking along the wall. They were picking their way barefoot across the sharp patches of wind-scraped rock. When they reached the end, they jumped with squeals and splashes into the water.

Bobby smiled. He could imagine the cold water folding itself around him. There was no better feeling. That moment of clear touch and sluggish sight. Then back into the world of air.

'That's what I should be doing,' he thought. 'I should be diving off the high wall, and hunting for baits and throwing fish heads at girls. Not Babe, of course. Other girls. Not killing seals.'

'Kill the stupid seal!' another part of him said. 'Kill it and don't make waves.'

"It's vermin. Kill it!" Dad and Grandad and Babe
and a hundred other voices shouted in Bobby's head.

Bobby heard the two youngsters giggling in
the distance, as they climbed the wall for another
jump. He longed to join them. Throw down the
family club, put on his old swimming togs and join
them.

But he couldn't. This summer a new phase of
his life would begin. He was a young man now.
Certain freedoms came with that, but also certain
responsibilities. He could stay up to watch action
movies, he could cycle five miles to the local disco,
he could even bring the boat out on his own around

the bay. But he also had to earn his keep, learn to

smoke and kill seals.

CHAPTER 8

All Hands on Deck

It seemed to Bobby as if he had been holding the club over his head for hours. The tendons in his arms sang like guitar strings. And the seal cub waited for the game to begin.

'I am stuck,' Bobby thought. 'Trapped in this position. I don't want to do this, but I have to.'

"You don't have to, son," a voice behind him said.

Bobby turned, the club still raised above his head.

His father was on the bank, squatting with his elbows on knees. His face was hard to read. Maybe understanding was there. Maybe disappointment too.

"I do have to, Dad," Bobby said. "I can too."

Brian Parrish shifted his weight. "I know you can, son," he said, "but you don't have to. Look."

Bobby's dad stood and shielded his eyes against the sun with a hand. He pointed a finger out into the bay.

Bobby turned seawards, and for several moments he could see nothing out of the ordinary. Then he noticed a wedge of light among the waves. At first he thought it was a sun shimmer, until it switched course three times in a second.

"Sprats," Bobby breathed.

"Yes," his dad said. "So, the mackerel are coming in. All hands on deck. Let's go."

The mackerel were coming in. For the first time in years. Bobby was off the hook, for now. And maybe, if the fish stayed for a few weeks, the bounty for a seal's flipper would be forgotten.

Bobby lowered the club and glanced down towards the seal cub. But there was only a wet stain on the rocks, drying as Bobby looked at it. The seal knew the fish were coming and he would be there to greet them, too.

"I'll take the boat out," Brian Parrish said. His tone was brisk. "I want you on the short wall with a line of feathers. Take a fishing box too, you'll need it."

Bobby nodded. He could fish. Killing fish was easier than killing seals. People ate fish.

"Get your brother down here too," Brian Parrish went on. "He could do with a couple of hours away from the books."

"Yes, Dad."

CHAPTER 9

Silver Blue

Bobby and his dad climbed over the stile into the quay itself. Nobody was walking anywhere. Everyone was scurrying.

'This must have been what it was like before an air raid in the War,' Bobby thought. 'Everyone has a job to do, and maybe not much time to do it in.'

Bobby took a moment to take in what was happening before he launched himself into the action.

The quay was thronged with locals searching for a good spot, like tourists around a luggage carousel in the airport. They carried lines and rods and containers of every kind. Buckets, washing baskets, pots and pans. All to be lowered into the spring tide. The sprats shimmered into the mouth of the dock like a sheet of sub-aqua chain mail, and behind them came the silver-blue flash of a million mackerel, driving themselves towards the dock in their greed.

As soon as the mackerel were in, they would be trapped by the simple maze of quay walls and only the lucky ones would escape. The locals had about three hours before the tide emptied the dock. Then any fish that remained would be piled high on the sand, and they would rot fast in the sun. Nobody wanted to eat rotting fish, so they had to be lifted fresh from the water. As many as possible. Later, the beached fish would be shovelled into salt and sold for fishmeal or bait.

Bobby's father clapped him on the arm. "Enough gawking," he said. "Get a move on."

"Right," Bobby said, and set off at a run down the quay. Something made him stop and look back. His father was watching him go with a lost look on his face.

"You are not me," that look said. "I thought you'd be a little me, but you are your own person."

Brian Parrish cupped a hand around his mouth. "Maybe we can talk later, about stuff," he called out. "You know – things, seal clubbing, whatever."

Bobby nodded. Was Dad prepared to let him be different then? Did Bobby want to be different?

Bobby turned and ran towards their house, calling for his little brother, for all Ferdia could not possibly hear him from so far away.

'I'll keep shouting,' Bobby thought. 'And Ferd will hear the second he's in range.'

Time was of the essence. Every second counted. Bobby pictured the feathers he would take and where they hung on the shed wall, so there would be no time wasted in deciding.

'I'll take the silver foil set,' he thought. They were his favourites. So realistic that, when they were in the water, even humans couldn't tell them apart from sprats.

The club bounced against his leg as he ran, and Bobby knew he would leave it in the shed and carry the feathers instead.

"The right tool for the right job," his grandad always said.

Maybe a club would work on a seal but it would be rubbish for catching fish.

Bobby looked sideways and saw the sea fizzing with sprats at the mouth of the dock. And flashing between them was his seal.

My seal? It's my seal now?

Bobby took a second to catch his breath and watched the seal's slick head as it darted in and out of the silver shoal.

'You should be thanking those fellows,' he thought. 'Not eating them.'

Those sprats had changed the seal's fate. If it wasn't for them, this day would have turned out very different for the cub.

'Those sprats changed my fate too,' Bobby realised. 'Thanks to them I get to be a boy for a while longer.'

Bobby took one last deep breath, then ran on towards the house.

"Ferdia!" he called. "Fer-deee-aaaaa."

About this book

This story is based on events which occurred during a summer of my father's youth in County Wexford, Ireland. It seems incredible these days that a bounty could be placed on seals, but at the time they were destroying the livelihoods of an entire fishing community. I remember wondering as my dad told me about the bounty whether or not I would be able to kill such a beautiful animal to save my father's job. This notion percolated in my mind for a long time and eventually came out in the form of this story – *The Seal's Fate*. To be honest, writing the story did not answer the question, "Could I do it?" Most of us will never be faced with a difficult choice like this, but many people are faced with life or death choices every day, and the choice that people make in that split second can change their lives for ever.

Eoin Colfer
Summer, 2015